Science Fiction Films

KATE HAYCOCK

Crestwood House
New York

Titles in this series

Adventure Films
Animated Films
Horror Films
Science Fiction Films

Words in **bold** appear in the glossary.

Cover: The magnificent spaceship that was used in the film *ET: The Extra-Terrestrial* (1982)

Series Editor: Deborah Elliott
Book Editor: Deborah Elliott
Designer: Helen White

First Crestwood House edition 1992
Copyright © 1991 Wayland (Publishers) Limited

Crestwood House
Macmillan Publishing Company
866 Third Avenue
New York, NY 10022

Macmillan Publishing Company is part of the Maxwell Communication Group of Companies.

First published in 1991 by Wayland (Publishers) Limited,
61 Western Road, Hove, East Sussex, England BN3 1JD

Library of Congress Cataloging-in-Publication Data
  Haycock, Kate.
    Science fiction films/Kate Haycock.
      p.   cm. — (Films)
    Includes bibliographical references and index.
    Summary: A history of science fiction films from George Méliès's earliest experiments at the beginning of the twentieth century to "Star Wars," "E.T.," and "Close Encounter of the Third Kind."
    ISBN 0-89686-716-1
    1. Science fiction films—History and criticism—Juvenile literature. [1. Science fiction films—History and criticism.
    2. Motion pictures—History and criticism.]   I. Title.   II. Series: Films (Crestwood House)
    PN1995.9.S26H33   1992
    791.43'656—dc20   91-31672
                                                         CIP
                                                         AC

Printed by G. Canale C.S.p.A., Turin, Italy

1 2 3 4 5 6 7 8 9 10

Contents

The strange unknown

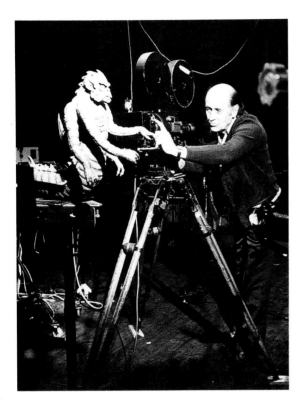

ABOVE **Special-effects expert Ray Harryhausen setting up his monster puppet in the film studio for *Clash of the Titans* (1981)**

LOOK up at the stars at night! Is there anyone out there? Is there life beyond our planet? If there is, what does it look like? Are the creatures friendly or hostile? Will they come and visit us? Might we, one day, go to visit them?

And what about the future? What will life be like on our own planet hundreds of years from now? Will machines and new inventions make life better or worse? How are they changing our lives now? There is so much we do not know.

Science fiction tries to predict or imagine the answers to questions like these. In the movies, these ideas can come to life.

Science fiction films have been popular ever since movie making began at the end of the nineteenth century. Some filmmakers were excited about the effects of science and technology on people's lives and looked forward to a kind of **Utopia**, an ideal world. Others were afraid of the power of machines and scientific discoveries and feared the end of the human race as they knew it.

In movies, it is possible to create a whole different world by using costumes, makeup, clever soundtracks, special sets or exotic locations.

Filmmakers also use a variety of tricks that are known as special effects. They make a film seem real and believable, so we are convinced that a spaceship is traveling through space or that a creature is devouring its victim.

Early special effects were very simple by today's standards, but even so they astounded movie audiences. Today, audiences expect special effects to be even more exciting and spectacular. Filmmakers spend a lot of money and take a long time to achieve the best possible results. Sometimes, however, filmmakers forget that a successful film must also have a good story and a high standard of acting. Without these, a film may **flop** miserably.

BELOW
The starship
Enterprise **was
created for the
Star Trek series of
films.**

On the moon

ABOVE **George Méliès's vision of the moon from his 1902 science fiction film *A Trip to the Moon*. Méliès used trick photography to produce brilliant special effects.**

ONE of the first science fiction filmmakers was a Frenchman named Georges Méliès. Méliès was a professional stage magician who was fascinated by the **illusions** that could be produced using trick photography. He made a film called *A Trip to the Moon* (1902).

In *A Trip to the Moon*, Méliès speeded up the film to give the audience the impression that the moon was getting closer as the explorers hurtled through space toward it. After they land, the explorers are captured by some strange **aliens**, but they are able to escape when they discover that the aliens disappear when hit. To produce this effect, Méliès used a technique called stop motion. He filmed the alien, then stopped the camera while the actor playing the alien stepped to one side. He then started the camera again — still focused on the place where the actor had been. When the film was run without a pause, it looked as if the alien had suddenly disappeared.

Travel to the moon was a popular idea in the first half of the twentieth century. A film called *Destination Moon* (1950), showing American astronauts landing on the moon, contained many clever effects. The specially constructed spaceship rotated so that the astronauts inside appeared to be walking across the walls and ceiling. This is what actually happens in space, where there is no **gravity**. The film won an **Oscar** for its special effects. These later proved to have been especially realistic when people were able to see actual pictures on television of the first moon landing in 1969.

Future worlds

ABOVE **The dark and depressing city of the future, featured in German director Fritz Lang's film** *Metropolis* **(1926). The film is still regarded as one of the finest examples of science fiction.**

WHILE some filmmakers came up with machines to take people into space, others were concerned about machines taking over our lives. In 1926, German film director Fritz Lang made a film called *Metropolis*. It is set in a huge city of the future. In this city, a small ruling class leads very comfortable lives, while the workers toil away in underground factories, their lives dominated by machines.

The film took over a year to make and cost a lot of money. There were 36,000 **extras**, including 1,100 bald men in one scene. There were also some extremely complicated special effects, including a new technique for shooting outdoor scenes. These were shot in the studio using filmed backgrounds.

Metropolis was a **silent film**, but the images of the future were very powerful, and the film is still admired today.

Many of us would like to travel into the future. In *The Time Machine* (1960), an inventor builds a machine that allows him to travel back and forth in time. While traveling quickly into the future, he sees a tree pass through all the seasons, losing its leaves in a matter of seconds.

In *Back to the Future* (1985), the character played by Michael J. Fox travels in a time machine back to the time when his parents first met. By interfering with the past, he almost prevents his own birth.

Comic strip heroes

MOVIES were very popular in the 1930s. Children used to go to the theater every Saturday to follow the exploits of their favorite heroes in the same way that we watch ours on television today.

One of the great heroes of this time was Flash Gordon. He was originally seen in a comic strip, and his adventures were made into three films: *Flash Gordon* (1936), *Flash Gordon's Trip to Mars* (1938) and *Flash Gordon Conquers the Universe* (1940).

Each film was divided into several weekly episodes, called serials. Flash and his fiancée, Dale Arden, go on a space mission to the planet Mongo. The emperor, Ming the Merciless, orders his troops to arrest them. As Flash and Dale try to escape, they encounter creatures such as shark men who live under water, clay people, hawk men who inhabit Sky City, and giant "orangapoids." Some are **hostile** and try to kill Flash and Dale, while some help them in their plight. Flash visits many planets and has many narrow escapes, but he always manages to survive to fight another day.

The exploits of another cartoon hero, Buck Rogers, appeared as a movie serial in 1939. Buck has been asleep for 500 years. He awakens to find the world threatened by Zuggs, who are invaders

ABOVE **Flash Gordon (left), the savior of the universe, together with his mortal enemy, Emperor Ming the Merciless. Flash was played by Buster Crabbe.**

from the planet Saturn. Buck springs into action against them and against the deadly enemy, Killer Kane. With exciting gadgets, hideous villains and secret passages, these films were a thrilling way to spend Saturday mornings.

Buck Rogers and Flash Gordon became popular again forty years later when they appeared in new films: *Buck Rogers in the 25th Century* (1979) and *Flash Gordon* (1980).

RIGHT **Buck Rogers first appeared as a movie serial in the 1930s. The character reappeared in 1979 in *Buck Rogers in the 25th Century*. American actor Gil Gerard, in the title role, continued the battle against Killer Kane.**

Meddling with science

A FEAR of science, and of the dangers of meddling with it, was a theme of many films in the 1940s and 1950s. People were particularly afraid of radiation, partly because they did not fully understand its powers. In a film called *Dr. Cyclops* (1940), a scientist uses radiation to reduce the size of wild animals. He gets carried away with his success and experiments on humans, shrinking them to a fraction of their size. The film used giant sets to make the actors seem tiny.

ABOVE **In *The Incredible Shrinking Man* (1957), special photographic methods were used to make 6-foot-tall actor Grant Williams "shrink" to less than an inch. In this scene he is trying to fend off his cat.**

In *The Incredible Shrinking Man* (1957), a man starts to shrink as a result of a radiation leak. He finds himself terrified of his own cat, which seems to have been transformed into a giant tiger, and he almost drowns when a pipe leaks. He becomes even more miniature and has an exhausting battle with a spider. He manages to overcome the creature by fighting it with a sewing needle, which is almost as big as he is.

Once again, most of the effects in this film were achieved by building giant sets so that the actor appeared to be gradually getting smaller. The battle scene with the spider was filmed in two parts — one part with the actor and one with a real spider. The films were then combined to make it look as if the spider were actually bigger than the actor.

ABOVE In *The Invisible Man* (1933), the actor in the title role appeared to be completely invisible underneath his clothes and bandages.

The power of radiation to change the shape and size of creatures has been used in many science fiction films. Giant ants in the film *Them!* (1954) and a spider in *Tarantula* (1955) are two examples.

In *The Invisible Man* (1933), a scientist discovers a drug that makes him invisible. At first he enjoys himself, but as he realizes the extent of his power, he becomes violent and even commits murder. Because he is invisible, no one can catch him.

One of the best effects in the film is when he removes all his clothes, to reveal that there is nothing underneath. For this scene, a stuntman undressed in front of a black cloth, wearing a black outfit under his clothes so that his body appeared invisible. A background was then added to the film.

Watch the skies!

IN THE 1950s, there were many reported sightings of unidentified flying objects (UFOs). They often appeared to be disk shaped and were therefore given the name of flying saucers. People wondered whether creatures from other planets were trying to make contact with us or perhaps trying to invade the Earth.

As no UFOs have ever landed (as far as we know), filmmakers started to imagine who or what was aboard them. With the help of special effects, they invented **extraterrestrial** beings that could take any shape or appearance and could possess any power or weakness.

BELOW **A scene from the 1951 version of** *The Thing*. **In the film, a blood-drinking alien is on the loose.**

ABOVE *The Thing* **was remade in 1982. The alien could take on any shape or form it liked — it could even take over humans. This made it much more frightening than in the 1951 version.**

In *The Day the Earth Stood Still* (1951), a giant silver flying saucer lands in a baseball park in the middle of Washington, D.C. One of the aliens aboard, Klaatu, looks like a human being and even speaks English. He is accompanied by a huge robot named Gort. They have come to warn people on Earth to stop developing nuclear weapons. Unfortunately, the government refuses to take any notice, and Klaatu is killed. He is brought back to life by Gort, and they fly off in their spaceship, with their mission unaccomplished.

The alien in *The Thing* (1951) is a survivor from a crashed UFO. It needs blood to feed its young and devours anyone in its path. Although the alien is finally exterminated, the radio warns everyone to be watchful. "Keep watching the skies!" is the alarming message. *The Thing* was remade in 1982. In this version, the alien was able to assume any shape whatsoever, and was therefore much harder to detect and capture.

In the 1979 film *Alien*, a creature is hiding on board a spaceship. The crew knows it is there but cannot find it. The tension builds. The film's poster said "In space no one can hear you scream." One of the more startling effects is when the alien, in snakelike form, explodes out of a crew member's stomach. In the **sequel**, *Aliens* (1986), the only surviving crew member returns to the alien planet after 57 years of deep sleep and encounters more of these hideous creatures.

There is an alien aboard the spacecraft in *Dark Star* (1974). This film was made on a very low budget but is considered an excellent example of its kind. It is partly a **spoof**, with an alien that resembles a "space hopper" and a crew starting to go crazy from having been in space for so long. There are some genuinely funny parts, including a talking bomb that keeps threatening to go off and has to be persuaded otherwise.

In some films, the aliens take ridiculous forms. In *Invasion of the Saucer Men* (1957), the aliens are green pygmies with **bloated** heads who kill by injecting poison through their fingernails.

In *The Blob* (1958), the alien is a big lump of red jelly. It arrives from outer space and eats humans, growing bigger all the time. First it takes over a supermarket and then a theater. It is stopped when the teenagers who discovered it finally convince the authorities to take action.

BELOW **Actor John Hurt discovers the pods containing the alien in the 1979 film *Alien*. Later, the unfortunate character played by Hurt has the creature explode out of his stomach.**

B-movies

ABOVE **The famous creature from** *Creature from the Black Lagoon* **(1954)**

SCIENCE fiction films were very popular in the 1950s. Because of this, film studios produced many of them very quickly and cheaply, sometimes with dreadful results. These **"B-movies"** often had very simple plots that were totally unbelievable. The acting was bad, and the cheap special effects were amusing because they were so obvious and ridiculous. The audience could see that there were wires making objects move or that the spaceships were only models.

Sometimes the best part of a B-movie was its title. Some particularly **ludicrous** ones were *Teenagers* *from Outer Space* (1959), *The Attack of the 50 Foot Woman* (1958) and *I Married a Monster from Outer Space* (1958). In 1978, a spoof film called *Attack of the Killer Tomatoes* came out. It had the title, the poor special effects and the awful acting of a typical 1950s B-movie.

For a while during the science fiction boom of the 1950s, audiences were thrilled by 3-D films. The three-dimensional process, or 3-D, made the images on the screen seem incredibly realistic. The disadvantage was that, to see the effects, the audience had to wear special glasses provided by the theater. The novelty soon wore off.

One of the most popular 3-D films was *Creature from the Black Lagoon* (1954). The creature is a **prehistoric** beast that can move about in water or on land. It is a sympathetic being that is captured by a group of explorers but escapes. It falls in love with one of the females in the group, however, and later kidnaps her.

Films with creatures emerging from under water were popular in the early 1950s. An atomic bomb test causes a giant octopus to emerge from the sea in *It Came from beneath the Sea* (1955). The octopus terrorizes the city of San Francisco. The low **budget** for this film meant that the model of the octopus was made with only five legs instead of eight like a real octopus.

BELOW **In the 1950s, 3-D films were very popular. Audiences wore special glasses that made some of the images in the films appear to jump off the screen.**

Beware the alien

ABOVE **The aliens are here! In the 1953 film *It Came from Outer Space*, an alien spaceship lands. Its occupants kidnap humans and replace them with robots.**

ALIENS that have huge heads, three eyes and make strange noises are frightening. But what if an alien is living among us and we don't even know? What if one of your friends at school or a member of your family is really an alien? In *Not of this Earth* (1957), a man appears to be normal until he removes his sunglasses. His eyes look like Ping-Pong balls, and we realize he is not human.

In the 3-D film *It Came from Outer Space* (1953), a spaceship lands in a remote desert in Arizona. The occupants kidnap humans to help them repair their ship. So that no one notices the humans are missing, the aliens replace them with exact **replicas.** The replicas look normal, but a few details give them away — for example, they are able to stare at the midday sun without blinking.

In *Invasion of the Body Snatchers* (1956), aliens take over people's bodies. They seem to be normal, apart from one thing — they have no human emotions. One by one, people realize that there is something strange about their friends or relatives. No one is able to recognize who is an alien and who isn't. By the end of the film, the town is in a state of **hysteria** caused by fear of who and what the aliens are and why they are there.

This film and others of its kind are successful because they show extraordinary things happening to ordinary people. You might be next!

BELOW *The Invasion of the Body Snatchers* **(1956) continued the theme of aliens arriving on Earth. In this film, the visitors assumed human bodies in an attempt to take over the world.**

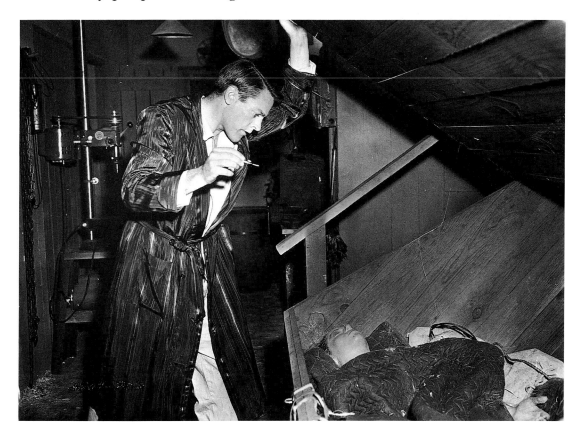

The evolution of humans

ABOVE **One of the incredible special effects featured in** *2001: A Space Odyssey* **(1968)**

ONE of the most spectacular science fiction films ever made was *2001: A Space Odyssey* (1968). This was a more serious film than many of the low-budget movies of the previous twenty years. The film was based on the book by Arthur C. Clarke, a well-known science fiction writer.

2001: A Space Odyssey is about the evolution of the human race. It spans four million years, from prehistoric times to the distant future. The film starts with ape-men learning how to make tools and weapons. It then moves into the future. A spaceship discovers that a rock on the moon is giving out signals. The computer on board the spaceship, HAL 9000, **malfunctions**, causing the death of all but one of the astronauts. The survivor sees his life flash before him and is then reborn.

Film buffs still argue over the meaning of the film, but the special effects were like nothing seen before. The director, Stanley Kubrick, spent $6.5 million on the sets and special effects alone. He paid attention to every detail. He used every known special effect and invented new ones, like the dazzling light show seen toward the end of the movie. More than twenty years later, the film is still one of the most visually spectacular ever made.

In *The Planet of the Apes* (1968), a group of astronauts lands on a planet that is run by apes. There are humans on the planet, but they are second-class citizens. After a series of adventures, one of the astronauts finds the Statue of Liberty buried in the sand. We realize that the planet is actually Earth, at some time in the distant future. The film's message is that, although we descend from apes, in the future they could rule over us.

LEFT *The Planet of the Apes* (1968) **was set on earth in the future. In the film, humans were ruled by apes.**

Let the Force be with you

ABOVE *Star Wars* (1977), directed by George Lucas, is one of the most popular science fiction films ever made.

IN 1977, two science fiction films broke box office records and became modern classics. One of these was *Star Wars*.

Star Wars cost $9 million to make, and most of this money was spent on special effects. There are realistic interplanetary wars featuring fleets of spaceships filmed by computer-controlled cameras. There are also dozens of weird and wonderful characters — both human and nonhuman — and extravagant costumes and sets.

The film's hero, Luke Skywalker, is called to rescue beautiful Princess Leia, who has been captured by the evil Darth Vader. Luke is accompanied by two robots called C-3PO and R2-D2, and he receives help from the Jedi knight Ben (Obi-Wan) Kenobi and the space pilot Han Solo. Luke's adventures take him to planets all over the universe, where he meets strange creatures. Some help him with his mission; some attack or capture him.

Luke and his friends rescue Princess Leia, but in the sequel, *The Empire Strikes Back* (1980), they are still under attack from Darth Vader. Darth Vader is a former Jedi knight who possesses the secret energy known as the Force. With his mechanical body parts and his terrifying appearance, he is a formidable opponent.

Luke's task is to fight Darth Vader. In preparation, he goes to the planet Dagobah to meet his teacher, Yoda. Yoda is a green gnome who trains him to use the lightsaber, the weapon of the Jedi knights.

The Star Wars story comes to an end in *Return of the Jedi* (1983), in which Luke finally meets Darth Vader unmasked, and the evil empire is destroyed.

While the Star Wars films were considered the best of the adventure films, others, such as the Star Trek films, *The Black Hole* (1979) and *Battlestar Galactica* (1977), were also popular.

BELOW **Jedi knight Darth Vader, the villain of the Star Wars series**

Close encounters

ABOVE **The beautiful "mother ship" from** *Close Encounters of the Third Kind* **(1977)**

THE other great film of 1977 was director Steven Spielberg's *Close Encounters of the Third Kind*. A close encounter of the third kind is contact with the occupants of a UFO.

A group of people who received signals from a UFO gather in a lonely spot to await its arrival. The crowd includes a mother whose son has disappeared.

They all watch as the beautiful "mother ship" slowly descends in a glow of bright lights. The

PREVIOUS PAGE **One of the amazing effects from** *ET: The Extra-Terrestrial,* **when Elliot and the lovable alien go for a bicycle ride with a difference.**

doors open. Dozens of human beings appear. Many are aircraft pilots whose planes had mysteriously disappeared without trace many years before. The missing boy is also among them, returning safely. The film's hero, a local repairman, is drawn inside the ship, and it disappears with him aboard.

Instead of the usual image of aliens as hostile beings, *Close Encounters* portrays them as harmless, intelligent creatures. The special effects are also excellent. In one clever scene, all the toys in a house come to life as the UFO passes over. The mother ship itself is spectacular, and the UFO landing site was the largest indoor set ever built.

Steven Spielberg's next film, *ET: The Extra-Terrestrial* (1982), features another friendly and harmless alien — the odd-looking ET. A young boy named Elliot finds ET, who has accidentally been left behind by his family after a visit to Earth. At first Elliot trusts only other children with his secret and hides ET in his bedroom.

More than anything, ET wants to go home and rejoin his family. "ET phone home," he continually repeats. Earth's pollution makes him sick, and he comes close to dying. However, Elliot and his friends finally manage to make contact with ET's people and urge them to come save ET. Elliot and ET have become very fond of each other. They hug with tears in their eyes as ET prepares to leave.

ET: The Extra-Terrestrial became the most popular film of all time only weeks after it was released. Steven Spielberg knew the importance of a good story, and the special effects, including ET himself, were superb. In one memorable scene ET teaches Elliot and his friends to fly, and they soar high over the town.

Robots and replicants

IN contrast to the fun and adventure of the Star Wars films and the warmth of the Spielberg stories, many recent science fiction films show a bleak future with very little to look forward to. The destruction of the Earth, bare landscapes and violent action are typical features of these films, and robots often play important parts.

In the Mad Max films, which are set in Australia, people no longer care about each other. There are gangs on motorcycles, and killings are common. In the first film, *Mad Max* (1979), a police officer finds his family murdered and sets out to find the killers.

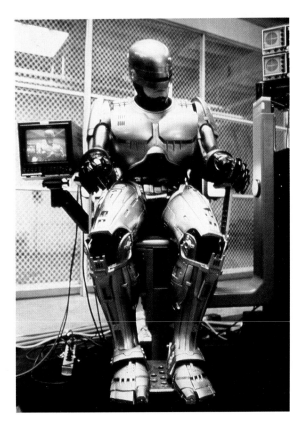

ABOVE **The incredible figure of the robot police officer in** *Robocop* **(1987)**

There is plenty of crime and violence in the future world of *Robocop* (1987). Robots hold many of the important jobs. A police officer is murdered and rebuilt as a robot — Robocop. Unlike real robots, however, he still has some human emotions and can remember the time when he was a human being.

The robot in *Terminator* (1984) has no emotions. He is a cold-hearted killer, played by the actor Arnold Schwarzenegger. He is indestructible: he can replace parts of his body if he is injured. In *Total Recall* (1990), Schwarzenegger plays a secret agent who goes to Mars in the year 2075 to find his memory and clashes violently with the Martian inhabitants.

In *Blade Runner* (1982), Earth has been ruined and most of the population has moved to other planets. A number of dangerous "replicants" remain among the people left on Earth. These replicants look like humans, but they have superhuman strength and are extremely intelligent. The actor Harrison Ford plays the police officer whose task it is to hunt them and destroy them.

Many people admire this film for its imaginative set, which shows Los Angeles in the year 2019. Space travel is common and the police drive "spinner cars" that move up and down in the sky.

In more than ninety years of science fiction films, some have already been proven wrong. Others have correctly predicted developments in science and space travel. We will have to wait to see whether the bleak predictions of the films mentioned in this chapter come true. Meanwhile the filmmakers continue to scare, excite and entertain us.

Glossary

Aliens Beings from another planet.

Bloated Swollen or puffed up.

B-movies Films that are made cheaply and quickly. They are often of poor quality.

Budget The amount of money spent on a film.

Extras Actors with small parts, often used in crowd scenes.

Extraterrestrial From beyond the Earth's atmosphere.

Film buffs People who know a lot about films.

Flop To fail, be unsuccessful.

Gravity The force that keeps us on the Earth.

Hostile Unfriendly.

Hysteria A state of panic, excitement or fear.

Illusions Tricks that make something seem real.

Ludicrous Laughable, ridiculous.

Malfunctions Goes wrong or does not work properly.

Oscar An award given to a filmmaker or actor for an outstanding achievement. Oscars are awarded each year in the United States.

Prehistoric From before recorded history began.

Replicas Exact copies.

Sequel A film that continues the story of a previous one.

Silent film A film in which the actors do not speak, made before the invention of the soundtrack in 1927.

Spoof A film that makes fun of other films.

Utopia An imaginary perfect world.

Further reading

Belgrano, Giovanni. *Let's Make a Movie.* New York: Scroll Press, 1973.

Cohen, Daniel. *Masters of Horror.* Boston: Houghton Mifflin, 1984.

Coynik, David. *Film: Real to Reel.* Evanston, Illinois: McDougal-Littell, 1976.

Ezmolian, John. *Lights! Camera! Scream! How to Make Your Own Monster Movie.* New York: Messner, 1983.

Hargrove, Jim. *Steven Spielberg: Amazing Filmmaker.* Chicago: Children's Press, 1988.

Schwartz, Perry. *Making Movies.* Minneapolis, Minnesota: Lerner, 1989.

Smith, Dian G. *American Filmmakers Today.* New York: Messner, 1983.

Smith, Dian G. *Great American Film Directors.* New York: Messner, 1987.

Staples, Terry. *Films and Videos.* New York: Warwick, 1986.

Tatchell, Judy and Cheryl Evans. *The Young Cartoonist.* Tulsa, Oklahoma: EDC, 1987.

Picture Acknowledgments

Aquarius Picture Library 4, 5, 8, 10, 11, 17, 20, 22;
The Kobal Collection 6, 7, 9, 12, 13, 14, 15, 16, 18, 19, 21, 23, 24, 25, 27, 28, 29.

Index